# Bella
# Donna

Ruth Symes thinks the next best thing to being magical is writing stories about magic. She lives in Bedfordshire, and when she isn't writing she can be found by the river walking her dogs, Traffy and Bella (who are often in the river).

Find out more at www.ruthsymes.com


Marion Lindsay has always loved stories and pictures, so it made perfect sense when she decided to become a children's book illustrator and won the Egmont Best New Talent Award. She lives and works in Cambridge, and in her spare time she paints glass and makes jewelry.

Find out more at www.marionlindsay.co.uk

# Bella Donna

Too Many Spells

### Ruth Symes

Illustrated by Marion Lindsay

Sky Pony Press
New York

Originally published in the UK in 2011 by Piccadilly Press Ltd., an
imprint of The Templar Company Plc.

10 9 8 7 6 5 4 3 2 1

Library of Congress Cataloging-in-Publication Data is available on file.

Cover design by Simon Davis
Cover illustration credit Marion Lindsay

Print ISBN: 978-1-63450-155-2
Ebook ISBN: 978-1-63450-611-3

Printed in the United States of America

# Chapter 1

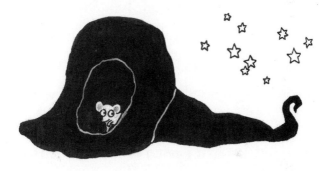

Some people might think that being a witch is easy-peasy, but that's where they'd be wrong. And I should know—I *am* a witch. Well, strictly speaking, I'm a witchling, which is a young, trainee witch.

Being a witchling can get very confusing. Before school and after school, every weekend, and school vacations, I spend my time in the magic world of Coven Road, but the rest of the time I have to go to school in the ordinary world.

I've only lived on Coven Road for a few months. I used to live at Templeton Children's Home—I was left on the doorstep there when I was a baby. I dreamed that one day I'd be adopted by someone who didn't mind that I wanted to be a witch—it was all that I've ever wanted to be. Then one day Lilith came to the children's home. I just knew she was special and I had to be adopted by her. Matron Harrigan, who is in charge of the children's home, said I could have a trial adoption to see how we got along, and that's when Lilith whisked me off to Coven Road.

I'd never have guessed, not for one second, when I was living at Templeton Children's Home that somewhere like Coven Road was so close. I say "road" but it's more of a crescent-shaped cul-de-sac with a garden in the center.

When it's being its magical self, none of the houses on Coven Road look the same. One house looks like a miniature Taj Mahal; another is balanced in a tree. Lilith and I live in a thatched cottage with roses that continually change color around the door. Zorelda, the Grand Sorceress, lives in a magnificent Ice Palace where we all go for parties and ceremonies. And there are unicorns in the garden at the center.

Coven Road is the most amazing place. Everyone who lives there is a witch—and it turned out that I didn't just want to be a witch, I actually *was* one too! Lilith had realized this as soon as she met me.

It's very important that all this remains a closely guarded secret from the outside world, so a spell is cast every month to protect Coven Road from harm. The spell makes sure Coven Road will look normal when non-witches come and visit and

means that non-witch passersby can't even see the entrance to it.

Everyone who lives on Coven Road has to make three promises. We have to promise never to use magic in the ordinary world. We have to promise never to bring anyone who isn't a witch to Coven Road without permission. And we have to promise that we will never, ever tell anyone outside Coven Road the truth about Coven Road—and that is *sooooo* hard! I live in the most exciting, magical place in the world and I can't even tell anyone at school about it. Apart from Sam, of course.

Sam is the closest I've got to a brother. He used to live at Templeton Children's Home like me, but then he was adopted by Tracey and Trevor, the owners of our local Woodland Wildlife Center. Luckily they're just as crazy about wildlife and mini-beasts as Sam is because he could never have gone to live with someone who wasn't an animal lover. It would have been just too hard for him.

Recently there was an accident and Sam discovered Coven Road. It was awful, but it all got figured out, and now Sam knows about me being a witchling and about the magic on Coven Road. He's promised not to tell anyone, and I know he will keep it a secret, and not just because Zorelda said something bad would happen if he didn't. Although knowing Sam, he'd probably really like it if she turned him into a toad or something!

I like animals as well. We have five cats at our house on Coven Road. Four of them live mainly on the bookshelves in the living room and don't like going outside. They're all Siamese cats and their names are Mystica, Bazeeta, Brimalkin, and Amelka. They do a lot of staring at people and don't like being petted very much. Then there's

Pegatha who loves being petted and likes just about everyone, apart from Lilith's niece Verity and the neighbor's dog, Waggy. Pegatha sleeps on my bed at night, and I think she is the best cat in the whole world.

My other friend at school is Angela. She's crazy about the color pink and I know she would love to see the new pink unicorn foal that's been born on Coven Road, but I can't bring her here to show it to her.

I sit next to Angela in class, and she's always trying to get me to wear pink like her. I, however, prefer to wear black.

"Some day you'll realize pink is your color," Angela keeps telling me.

I don't think I will. Whoever heard of a *pink* witch? Not that I can say that to her, of course.

One of the best things about being a witchling is learning how to cast spells. I wish regular

schoolwork was as easy, but it isn't. I seem to have a mental block when it comes to math—especially algebra. One day I drew a giant X over my test paper because I couldn't understand it, and it made my teacher, Mrs. Pearce, really angry.

"Well," said Mrs. Pearce, when she saw what I'd done, "you'll have to try harder than that, won't you, Bella Donna?"

I wasn't sure if I should nod my head, because I agreed I would have to try harder, or shake my head because I had been trying very hard indeed.

"You can retake the test tomorrow during lunch," Mrs. Pearce said.

If only I was able to do magic at school, everything would be so much easier. There must be a spell I could learn for making a test fill in its own correct answers.

"You okay, Bella Donna?" Lilith asked me when I got home.

Lilith is the most fantastic mom ever, at least as far as I'm concerned. She's always got time for me and is interested in what I do and she's fantastic at spells and makes the most delicious food ever.

We recently had a talk about how I could tell her anything, even things I thought she might not want to hear. I do try, but when you haven't been used to having anyone to tell, it can be hard. I try to be the best daughter I can and make her proud of me and not give her too much to worry about.

"Fine," I said. But I

wasn't really fine. Not fine at all. I was worrying about the next day and the test I was going to have to retake. I'd have told Lilith if I'd thought she'd be able to help, but I didn't really see how she could—other than making Mrs. Pearce disappear, of course. I didn't think Lilith would agree to do that. No witch would ever use magic outside Coven Road unless it was for a really, really good reason—a life-and-death sort of reason. Even I had to admit my algebra test wasn't a life-and-death situation.

I expect there was a spell to make Mrs. Pearce vanish. There's a spell for just about everything. I'm a very new witchling and I didn't know a spell that did that, even if I was allowed to use it—which I knew I wasn't. It didn't stop me thinking about it, though. I didn't need Mrs. Pearce to vanish for long—a few days, or a week, or maybe two weeks at the most. Just long enough for her to have forgotten about the test. Even if I did make her vanish I wouldn't make her invisible so she'd be wandering around all scared and ghostlike. She only had to disappear from school, so I could send her off for a little vacation somewhere.

I went into my room and opened my math book. I knew I should be studying it, but instead I tried to imagine the sort of vacation Mrs. Pearce might like. A vacation on the beach? I tried to imagine Mrs. Pearce surfing through the waves, but it didn't feel quite right. Maybe she'd like to visit the pyramids or go on a safari and meet baby elephants. But what if she didn't forget about the test and still expected me to do it when she came back?

In fact, I didn't even need to make her vanish, just forgetful, and I knew there was a spell for that.

"What's your face all scrunched up for?"

Verity said, coming into my room.

Verity is Lilith's niece. She's a few years older than me and the only other witchling on Coven Road. She's always coming over to our house after school because her mom works late and I think she gets lonely.

Verity's been banned from doing any magic because she cast a spell when she wasn't supposed to. That was when I first came to live on Coven Road and she used magic to try to get me into a whole heap of serious trouble. Now I know that she did it because she was jealous of me, but I'm not very sure how I feel about her.

"I was just thinking," I said.

"Thinking about what?"

"If I could do a spell to make someone forget something."

Verity was curious. "Make who forget what?"

I almost told her
but Verity isn't very
trustworthy, and I didn't
want her to tell Lilith.

"Oh nothing. Doesn't
matter."

We went downstairs
and switched on the
TV to the Broomstick
channel. It was time
for our favorite
program.

Pegatha came into
the room and hissed
at Verity. Verity
doesn't like Pegatha,
and Pegatha doesn't
like her, but I like
Pegatha very much.

The words WITCHLING SPELL-CASTING CONTEST flashed up on the TV with lots of gold stars that whizzed around the screen and then bounced out of the set completely! Pegatha raced around the room chasing after them but she couldn't catch any.

One of the presenters, Haggerty, came onto the screen. She was very round and dressed in black.

"Could you be this year's Spell-Casting Champion?" she said. "Well, could you?"

The other presenter, Fizzwart, pushed Haggerty out of the way. Fizzwart was very thin and dressed in green. "Are you a witchling looking for excitement and adventure?" she said. "Are you?"

Both Haggerty and Fizzwart were dressed as pretend witches in pointy hats and cloaks. Real witches are usually much more attractive and have much better clothes. They stood side by side and spoke together. "Then enter the Witchling spell-casting contest!" they said, and they pointed their fingers at me.

The thing with Broomstick TV that's different from any other TV channel is that you can talk to the TV, and it can talk back to you, and it can see you too.

"Come on, Bella Donna," said Haggerty.

"You know you want to," said Fizzwart.

And they were right—in a way I did want to. I wanted to make Lilith proud of me. I wanted to see her smiling face when I won the spell-casting contest.

"I meant to enter that this year," Verity said.

"But you're not allowed to use magic, are you, Verity?" said Haggerty, and she laughed her trademark cackle that she put on for the show.

"Naughty, naughty, naughty!" shrieked Fizzwart.

Just because Verity couldn't enter the contest didn't mean *I* couldn't enter it. Lilith would be so proud of me if I won it—she probably wouldn't even care if I wasn't good at algebra!

"Do they have it every year?" I asked Verity.

"Yes," she said. "It's only for witchlings between the ages of ten and thirteen. I'll be fourteen on Halloween, so this would have been my last chance to enter." She looked sad.

"I expect you have to know lots of spells," I said. I hadn't been a witchling for long enough to know many spells.

Verity shook her head. "That's not how it works. It's not about how many spells you can cast—otherwise the oldest witchlings would always win. It's about how well you cast a spell."

I didn't know many spells but so far the ones that I did know had worked extremely well.

"Are you really thinking of entering it?" Verity asked.

Sometimes it's hard to know when Verity is joking and when she's being serious.

"I mean, you haven't been learning for very long . . ."

That was true. I probably wouldn't stand a chance.

". . . but you do seem to have some natural talent."

I could hardly believe my ears. It was the nicest thing Verity had ever said to me.

I'm not good at most of my subjects at school, and I'm not good at sports, and when I sing my voice goes all wobbly. Spell-casting is the only thing I've ever been any good at. But I wasn't sure. Maybe I wouldn't stand a chance. Maybe I wouldn't even get through the first round.

"Perhaps," I said.

A muslin pouch flew out of the TV screen

and landed, *plonk*, in my lap.

"Here, see if you can cast this spell," Haggerty said. "If you can, you'll be in to win."

"But no cheating, Bella Donna," said Fizzwart. "It has to be all your own work."

I stared down at the pouch.

"So?" said Verity. "Are you going to enter?"

"I don't know," I said. I had the pouch of ingredients but that didn't mean I had to use it.

Verity let out a big sigh.

Verity and I didn't talk any more about the spell-casting contest or the forgetting spell, but that night I put the muslin pouch under my pillow and I had a dream that I won the spell-casting contest. I was given a gold cup and there was a magical witches' party to celebrate, and Lilith was very, very proud of me and Mrs. Pearce went far, far away to somewhere called the End of the Earth and lived in an igloo with a friendly moose for company.

# Chapter 2

I didn't want to go to school the next day. I told Lilith I had a sore throat, but she just gave me some hot water with honey and lemon to drink and said she was sure I'd feel better soon. You might think witches use magic all the time and could easily magic away a sore throat, but we never use magic for everyday things like that. Plus, I'm not sure Lilith really believed I had a sore throat anyway.

I walked to school as slowly as I could, but I still got there before the bell rang. Everyone else at school seemed very happy, but then, they would—they didn't have to stay in and redo a test at lunchtime.

I sat next to Angela, as usual, and looked at the front of the room. Mrs. Pearce's desk was empty. Something wasn't right. Mrs. Pearce was usually—no, *always*—there when we came in, but not today. Could Mrs. Pearce be late? But she was never late. Could Mrs. Pearce be sick? Mrs. Pearce was never sick.

I had a worried knot in my stomach. Had I somehow magicked her away? I'd so not wanted to take the test. I hadn't put a spell on her on purpose, but what if I'd put one on her by mistake? What if I'd done it when I was asleep and dreaming she was far, far away?

An important lesson for all witchlings to learn is how to control your power, because sometimes you can really want something to happen and then find out it has happened, without you even casting a spell, which can cause all sorts of problems. Once, before I went to live with Lilith and learned about my powers, before I even knew I was a witch, I'd wished someone would get a warty nose, and they did!

But I hadn't cast a spell without knowing I'd cast one for a long time. I thought I'd outgrown that stage. I really, really didn't want to have magicked Mrs. Pearce away by mistake—that was the sign of a very inexperienced witchling. Certainly not one that would win the Witchling spell-casting contest.

Our class got louder and louder as everyone began to realize Mrs. Pearce wasn't there. Some people even started flying paper planes and hardly anyone was sitting at their desk when the principal came in.

Behind her was a beautiful lady with long red hair—so long it went all the way down to her waist.

Everyone scrambled to sit back in their proper places.

"Now, children," the principal said. "Unfortunately, Mrs. Pearce can't be here today so you're going to have Miss Rowan as your teacher instead."

Sam put his hand up. "What's the matter with Mrs. Pearce?" he said.

The principal didn't seem to hear him. "So I'm sure you'll all make her feel very welcome and be on your best behavior," she continued.

"What's wrong with Mrs. Pearce?" Sam asked again. "Is she sick? Did she have an accident? Has she won the lottery?"

The principal made an angry face at Sam. "Stop being such a nosy boy," she said. "I told you, she's not here." The principal stomped out of the classroom.

Miss Rowan smiled at all of us. She looked so pretty and kind that I couldn't help but smile back. The rest of the class was smiling too. Everyone, that is, except Sam, who was scowling. I gave him a hard stare to tell him to be polite, but he was too busy scowling to notice.

"I'm very pleased to meet you all," Miss Rowan said. "I'm sure we are going to get along just fine."

She started to take attendance and, as usual, we each put our hand up as our name was called out.

"Angela . . ."

"Yes, Miss Rowan."

"Rajni . . ."

"Yes, Miss Rowan."

"Sam . . ."

"I'm over here," Sam said.

"So you are." Miss Rowan smiled sweetly at him. "I'll remember to keep an eye on you, Sam. A very watchful eye."

"And where's Bella Donna?" Miss Rowan asked.

Everyone looked around and stared at me.

I was sure I must have done something wrong, but Miss Rowan was smiling at me. I was feeling very, very confused.

I slowly put my hand up, and Miss Rowan gave me an even bigger smile.

"Ah, there you are. I should have guessed by your clothes," she said.

"She always wears black, Miss, no matter how often I tell her pink's better," Angela said.

I gave Angela a nudge, but she just continued.

"Don't mind her clothes—she's actually a very sweet girl," she told our new teacher.

If I'd been allowed to use magic outside Coven Road, Angela would have been croaking in her new frog body by now. I was definitely, absolutely, *not* sweet!

For the first part of the morning we had English, which I liked.

Then, the last lesson before lunch,

Miss Rowan said the dreaded words: "Time for some algebra."

I stared at the numbers

and letters but they made no sense to me at all. I stared at them so hard they started swimming around in front of my eyes. I couldn't go on like this. I had to do something.

As always, everyone else hurried out of the classroom as fast as they could go as soon as the lunch bell rang. But not me. I decided to tell Miss Rowan the truth.

"Is something wrong, Bella Donna?" Miss Rowan asked.

"I don't really understand algebra," I said in a very small voice.

Miss Rowan smiled. "Lots of people don't, but it's easy once you get the hang of it. Here—I'll show you."

And she did! As she wrote some of the equations out again and talked me through it, all of a sudden it started to make sense! The more she showed me and explained it the more sense it made. Very soon algebra made total sense!

"Thank you so much," I said.

"Not a problem at all," Miss Rowan replied.

"I can see you're a very talented, clever girl, and I'd like to help you as much as I can."

Talented? Clever? No teacher at school had ever called me either of those things before. Miss Rowan really was different. I thought Miss Rowan must be the best teacher in the whole world.

I went out onto the playground to join my friends.

"There's something weird about her," Sam said.

"Who?" I asked him.

"Our new teacher."

"What are you talking about?" I said. "She's not weird—*you're* weird."

"Well, she looks really mean," he said.

"No she doesn't, she looks really kind," said Angela.

"And she's funny," said Rajni. "She made me laugh."

"So why was she sneering all the time?" Sam said.

Sneering? I shook my head. I hadn't seen Miss Rowan sneer once. She'd been smiling all morning.

I was going to tell Lilith all about the new teacher and my worries that Mrs. Pearce had left

when I wanted her to. But when I got home Lilith was adding ingredients to the cauldron for a new spell she was working on. Spell-casting is a very serious business and it's important to concentrate, so I didn't want to interrupt her.

I went upstairs where I found Pegatha laying in her favorite place on my bed, waiting for me.

"Hello, Pegatha," I said. "Did you have a lovely sleepy day? Or have you been out catching mice?"

Pegatha just purred. Even though we live in magical Coven Road, Pegatha can't talk. She just makes normal cat sounds. Sometimes I wonder what she'd say if she could speak. She'd probably have lots of interesting things to tell me.

Her paws were resting on the strings from the spell-casting pouch that was still hidden under my pillow.

I'm not sure why I hadn't told Lilith about it. I think I was a bit embarrassed about wanting to enter the contest. What if I did really badly? What if I came in last? Lilith wouldn't be proud of me then.

# Chapter 3

Saturday is my favorite day of the week because I have my spell-casting lesson with Lilith, and spell-casting is just about the most exciting thing in the world. It used to always be me and Verity at Lilith's spell-casting classes but then

Verity got banned from using magic so now it's usually just me and Lilith.

Verity still comes along sometimes, although she's not allowed to do any spell-casting. Lilith says Verity's trying very hard to be a good witchling even if it isn't always easy for her. I don't mind when she comes to the lesson, really, but my favorite spell-casting lessons are when it's just me and Lilith.

Verity is a few years older than me and so she knows lots more spells than  I do. Witchlings can only start learning spells when they are ten years old and they're only allowed to learn one new spell a week at the most. You're not allowed to learn more than one a week because it would be too dangerous if you got the spells muddled up by mistake—which could easily happen if you learned too many too quickly.

Lilith says I'm doing really well and that I'm a natural when it comes to spell-casting. Most witchlings take nearly a month to learn a new spell, but so far it hasn't taken me nearly that long. In fact, I'm catching up with Verity, which was part of the reason why she was jealous of me.

Today we revised how to alter the colors of inanimate objects. I changed our sofa from cream to green to yellow to spotted to striped and then back again. Our cushions and curtains continued to change colors too. It was a fun spell that I'd first learned two weeks ago, and it made decorating really easy. Lilith and I could change the color of our house furnishings whenever we wanted to.

"Did Bella Donna tell you about the Witchling spell-casting contest?" big-mouth Verity asked Lilith halfway through the lesson.

"No," said Lilith, and she looked over at me. "Why didn't you—?"

"Haggerty and Fizzwart threw her a pouch of ingredients to cast a spell," Verity told Lilith. Then she turned to me. "You haven't even done it yet, have you?"

"Is this true?" Lilith asked me. She sounded surprised.

"Yes," I said in a small voice.

"And you didn't tell me?" Lilith looked disappointed.

"Sorry."

Verity could be a real pest sometimes. I should have told Lilith before. I knew I should have, but I wanted to wait until I'd decided whether to take part or not.

"Where is this pouch?" Lilith asked me.

"Under my pillow."

"Haggerty and Fizzwart told me to tell Bella Donna to hurry up if she wanted to enter," Verity said. "They also threw this through the TV screen for you to sign, Auntie Lilith."

Verity pulled a leaflet about the Witchling spell-casting contest from her pocket. It had an official application form on the back.

"Do you want to enter it, Bella Donna?" Lilith asked me. "Really? You've only been training as a witchling for a few months." Lilith didn't look as excited about the contest as I thought she would. In fact, she didn't look excited at all.

The contest had sounded exciting and I do love casting spells. Only I wasn't sure if I was good enough, and I really, really didn't want to come in last place.

"Um . . ."

"Maybe you shouldn't enter it," Verity said. "Every witchling in the country will be entering, so it would be difficult to win."

She was right, but instead of turning me off, Verity's words made me want to enter the contest more. I felt sure Verity wouldn't have said I shouldn't enter unless she thought I could win.

I picked up the leaflet. "Maybe . . ."

"If I'd still been allowed to use magic then I might have had a fighting chance," Verity said sadly.

The leaflet said the finale of the contest would be broadcast on Broomstick TV and the winner would receive a gold cup with the words BEST WITCHLING SPELL-CASTER and the date on it.

There was a space next to Mystica on the bookshelf that would be perfect for a spell-caster champion's cup.

The phone rang and Lilith went to answer it while I made up my mind.

"I could help you practice and learn things," Verity said.

"Could you?"

Verity had a lot more experience at spell-casting than I did.

She'd have had even more if she hadn't tried to get me banished from Coven Road, and been banned from using magic when everyone found out. Still, I was sure I would do a lot better if Verity tried to help me than if she didn't.

"How do I know I can trust you?" I said.

Verity smiled her most winning smile. "Because I'm your cousin and your friend, of course. And . . . I want to help, to make up for having been mean to you before."

That sounded nice of her, but could Verity really be trusted? Could I be absolutely sure she wouldn't ruin everything if she got a chance?

There was one thing I did know for sure, though, and that was that I wanted Lilith to be proud of me, and so I decided that I did want to enter the Witchling spell-casting contest. And I didn't just want to enter it—I wanted to win.

Lilith came back in. "It's your mom. She's going to take you out for lunch," she told Verity.

Verity was out of our house in a flash.

"Verity said she'd help me if I entered the contest," I told Lilith.

"Did she?" Lilith said, sounding surprised.

"I'm not sure I can trust her," I said. "But I

think I should try."

Lilith smiled and gave me a hug. "You really are amazing, Bella Donna," she said.

I didn't think she should say I was amazing until I'd done something amazing. "I haven't even entered the contest yet!" I said.

Lilith only laughed and shook her head. "That's not why you're amazing."

Lilith and I practiced a new spell that changed how foods tasted for the rest of the lesson. It was strange eating a slice of apple that tasted like chocolate and drinking a glass of milk that tasted exactly like orange juice.

I bet Pegatha would have been really confused if we'd let her have the piece of fish that tasted like strawberries, but we didn't let her have it because it wouldn't have been fair to her.

"The spell-casting contest will be an awful lot of hard work," Lilith said, when we were clearing up at the end of the lessson.

"I don't mind hard work."

Lilith looked doubtful. "What about your schoolwork?"

"I can manage that too."

"Okay, let's read the rules properly and then you can decide."

I found the leaflet and we sat on the sofa to read it together. Pegatha sat on the sofa with us and tried to read the leaflet, too, but we were careful she didn't scratch it with her little cat claws.

The spell-casting contest had three rounds. The first round, which any witchling could enter, was really the audition round. We'd all be given a pouch—as I had been—of ingredients and needed to cast a spell using these ingredients. Thirteen witchlings would then be selected to go on to the second round. This was a quiz round where we'd be tested on all sorts of ingredients. Three witchlings would then move forward to the third and final round. In this last round those witchlings that had survived the first two rounds would get to use their own ingredients to cast their very best spell.

In big red letters it said what Verity had already told me—that it was the QUALITY of our spell-casting that mattered and younger witchlings would not be penalized because they knew fewer spells than the older witchlings.

The more I read the leaflet, the more excited I became, and the more I wanted to enter the contest.

"Do you want me to fill in this application form or not?" Lilith asked me.

"I want you to."

"You're a very new witchling and it's going to be an awful lot of work," she told me again.

I nodded.

"You'll have to work hard to learn about all the ingredients, and you haven't had much experience practicing the spells . . ." she continued.

I still wanted to enter and passed Lilith a pen.

I didn't care about hard work and it'd be witchling work, anyway, not regular schoolwork. Spell-casting was too much fun to be called hard work. And I really wanted to see Lilith's smiling face when I won the spell-casting cup. If I won it.

"Maybe you should wait until next year," Lilith said. "I don't want you to be discouraged if you don't do well. You've got lots of natural talent and enthusiasm, but you've just started spell-casting and you'll be competing against witchlings who've had much more practice than you."

But I didn't want to wait—I wanted to make Lilith proud of me *now*.

Lilith sighed. "If you've really set your heart on
it then I'll help you as much as I can," she said. "I

just don't want you to get your hopes up and be disappointed. You're absolutely sure about this?"

"Absolutely."

"All right." She filled in the form and signed it at the bottom with a big flourishy squiggle and she stamped the form with her special witch's seal beneath her signature. Then something very strange happened—the form vanished into thin air. One second it was there, and the next second it was gone. I still found things like this amazing!

"What happens next?" I asked.

"You need to cast the admission spell with the pouch you were given. I can't help you with that, but there's a cauldron ready in the kitchen if you want to do the spell now."

I hugged Lilith, then picked up the pouch of ingredients and went to the kitchen before I could get too nervous. I opened the soft material of the pouch.

Inside I found five sunflower seeds, a small gold candle, a black pebble, six dried juniper berries, and a scattering of yellow rose petals. There was also a tiny scroll of paper with instructions on it, written in green ink:

Merry Meet, Witchling,
Welcome to the spell-casting contest.
Your task is to light the candle and mix
the ingredients in your cauldron while
chanting the words below.

I lit the candle and dumped the rest of the ingredients into the cauldron, which I then placed over the fire, just as Lilith had taught me. Then I stirred and chanted the words on the scroll, which wasn't easy because I didn't know if I was pronouncing them right or not.

"*Muzzuula ree muzzuula ra, muzula muzzuula muzula muzar.*"

And that was it! Nothing happened, besides a small blue bee flying out of the cauldron and then buzzing its way out through the window. Perhaps that was all that was supposed to happen. It wasn't a spell I'd done before. I wouldn't be sure until I heard from Haggerty and Fizzwart if I'd been selected or not.

I jumped when Lilith came into the kitchen. "Done?" she asked me.

"Done," I said. "But I don't know if I did it right. I thought I might hear right away from Haggerty or Fizzwart." I told Lilith about the blue bee, and Lilith looked at the instructions scroll.

"It's a spell to test your magical aptitude," she said.

"What's that?"

"Your potential."

"Oh."

Lilith knelt down beside me. "I think you might have heard immediately if . . ."

She didn't need to say any more. It looked like I hadn't been chosen.

I let her hug me and try to distract me by talking about a recipe she was going to do for dinner. I tried not to be too disappointed. But I was.

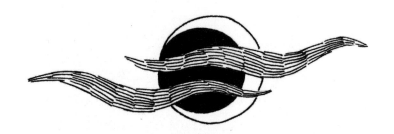

# Chapter 4

"Today we are going to be looking at different habitats," Miss Rowan said on Monday morning.

We started off by looking at the different types of places that animals live in. Then we had a quiz where we had to match the animal to the habitat. Zebras, lions, hippos, ostriches, and elephants live on the African plains. Polar bears live in the Arctic and penguins live in the Antarctic. They don't ever live together.

"They're always together on TV," Angela said.

Miss Rowan smiled. "Yes, but TV isn't always right," she told us.

The snow leopard doesn't live in the Arctic or the Antarctic; it lives in the Central Asian mountain ranges from China to the Himalayas, where it still gets very cold. On the fact sheet it said snow leopards sometimes wrap their long tails around their heads to keep warm. I imagined Pegatha having to do that. I didn't think she would like being that cold!

After break, Miss Rowan got out the colored pencils and some paper. "I want you to draw a picture of somewhere you'd like to live," she said.

"It can be anywhere you like—a castle or a cave . . ."

"I wouldn't want to live in a cave," Angela said.

"You would if you were a dragon or a bear," said Sam.

"Anywhere at all," said Miss Rowan.

We all got busy drawing. I didn't want to draw a pretend place. I thought where I lived was about as perfect as it could be. So I drew a picture of our magical house with different colored roses around the door, and with me and Lilith and Pegatha in the front yard.

I was going to draw Bazeeta, Mystica, Brimalkin, and Amelka, too, but they're always inside on the bookshelves, so I decided not to.

Miss Rowan came around our class to see how we were all doing.

"Very nice," she said when she saw mine.

"Thanks."

"And who is this?"

"That's Lilith."

"And what is the cat's name?"

"This one is Pegatha," I said, pointing to Pegatha in the front yard. Then I told her about the four others that hardly ever went outside.

Sam had drawn the Woodland Wildlife Center but given it lots more exotic animals than it really had.

"Is that a kangaroo?" Miss Rowan asked.

Sam nodded.

"What's that?"

"A *T. rex*. You should come and visit the Woodland Wildlife Center, Miss Rowan. Trevor said any time our class wanted to have a field trip we'd be more than welcome to spend the day there."

"Did he really?" said Miss Rowan.

"We live in a log cabin," Sam said. "It's got solar power so that we don't use too much non-renewable energy. Tracey says we have to be more environmentally aware. You should see the worm house I made with Trevor and Tracey. It was really good. It has about a hundred worms inside it, all wriggling around."

It was the most I'd ever heard Sam say to Miss
Rowan. Sam still didn't like her for some reason,
and he was usually very quiet, at least for him,
when she was around. But he was so proud of
his new parents and his new home that he took
any opportunity to talk about them.

Miss Rowan didn't say anything back, though,
and moved on to Angela. Angela had drawn a
huge pink house with six twirling pink turrets
and pink flags flying on each one.

"How lovely!" she said to her.

"I should have guessed you'd want to live in a
pink house," I said to Angela, as we waited with
our trays in the lunch line. Angela's real house
is brick with a white front door. The walls of
Angela's room are painted pink and her bed's got
a soft pink comforter too.

"I like pink," she said, which was the understatement of the year.

Miss Rowan was standing just behind us, making sure we all lined up without a fuss.

"Hurry up, Sam," she said.

As we got closer to the serving area, we could see it was apple pie for dessert. Angela didn't like apple pie.

"Oh, how I wish it were pink custard and pink sponge cake for dessert," Angela said dreamily.

And because Angela's my friend I said, "Me too," although I actually prefer chocolate pudding.

Then something very strange happened. The dinner lady came out of the kitchen with a baking tray full of pink sponge cake in one hand and a jug of pink custard in the other hand. She seemed a bit surprised herself when she put it down.

That was strange. I hoped it wasn't my fault,

that I hadn't magically made the pink sponge cake and custard appear by mistake. Could I have cast a spell without meaning to? I'd done it before, but I thought I had it under control now.

I didn't even want pink sponge cake and custard all that much. I'd just been saying it because I knew how much Angela liked it. If I'd used a spell by accident to conjure up dessert, surely I'd have got my favorite—chocolate tart? It didn't make sense. Maybe it was just coincidence.

"Enjoy your dessert," Miss Rowan said, as we walked past her with our trays.

"We will!" said Angela.

"Maybe I am a bit of a pink-fiend," Angela said, as she ate another mouthful of pink sponge cake.

"I like you being a pink-fiend," I said, smiling.

"Do you?"

"Yes."

"Then you're not ashamed of being my

friend?" she asked quietly.

Ashamed? What was she talking about? "Of course not. Why would you think that?"

Angela made a face. "How many times have you been to my house?"

"Lots?" I said.

"How many, exactly?"

I had to think. "Six?"

Angela nodded her head. "Six," she said. "How many times have I been to yours?"

"Ummm . . ."

Angela hadn't ever been to Coven Road. We had to get permission from Zorelda, the Grand Sorceress, before non-witches were allowed in.

Angela looked sad. "Not even once. Not even one tiny little visit."

I felt really bad. I hadn't realized how not being invited to my house might have made Angela feel before. My witch life was so separate and different

from my school life that I hadn't even thought about it. She wouldn't be able to see Coven Road in its magical form, of course, but she could still come over and meet Pegatha (who I was always talking about) and the other cats and Lilith.

"There is definitely something fishy about her," Sam said after lunch, when we were all out in the playground.

"Who?"

"Miss Rowan, of course. You must have noticed."

I hadn't noticed nor had anyone else. To the rest of us, Miss Rowan seemed the perfect teacher, and we told him so.

Just then, the bell rang for afternoon lessons and we hurried back to class.

"Maybe he's just jealous," Angela said when we were sitting at our desk.

"But why?" I said.

"Well, have you noticed how Miss Rowan does seem to be nicer to all of us than she is to him?"

I hadn't noticed really. Miss Rowan seemed to be nice to everyone as far as I could see.

Miss Rowan must've really liked the homes

project we did in the morning because in the afternoon she got out a big map showing our town and got us to put round red stickers on the roads we lived in.

When it came to my turn, I couldn't find Coven Road anywhere on the map and even though Miss Rowan tried to help me, she couldn't find it anywhere either, nor could any-one else.

"How very strange," Miss Rowan said.

"Must've been left out," I said.

But when Miss Rowan brought in another map, it wasn't on that one, either.

"It's just about here," I said, pointing to a green area of forest on the map where Coven Road should have been but wasn't.

I asked Lilith why Coven Road wasn't on any map when I got home. She said when we cast the spell at midnight once a month to stop non-witches from seeing the true Coven Road, it must also stop it from being seen on maps.

"It sounds like an extra something Zorelda has added," she said. "She really is quite amazing, you know. We're so lucky to have her as Coven Road's Grand Sorceress."

I asked Lilith if it was okay for Angela to come over.

"Of course. We'll just need to get permission from Zorelda. When would she like to come?"

I called Angela to see.

"Lilith says you can come over whenever you like. When would you like to come?"

"Tomorrow," Angela said. She sounded very excited.

Lilith said she'd check with Zorelda but she was sure tomorrow would be fine.

While Lilith called Zorelda to make the arrangements, I went into the living room and switched on Broomstick TV.

Haggerty and Fizzwart were there, talking about the history of the thirteen covens.

I decided to ask them if I'd been selected for the spell-casting contest, even though I knew I'd

probably have heard already if I'd been successful.

"You'll have to wait and see," Haggerty said when I finally mustered up courage.

"Patience is a virtue," shrieked Fizzwart.

That sounded as if they hadn't told anyone yet. A little glimmer of hope flickered inside me. Maybe I did have a chance after all. I tried to tell myself I didn't care if I were in it or not, but that wasn't true. I desperately wanted to be in the contest. The longer I had to wait, the more badly I wanted to be one of the witchlings who was chosen.

# Chapter 5

Sam was beaming as I went into class the next morning.

"What is it?" I asked him.

Before he could tell me, Miss Rowan made an announcement.

"As part of our homes and habitats project, we are going to be visiting the Woodland Wildlife Center tomorrow," she said, smiling.

Now I knew what Sam was so happy about. He loved Trevor and Tracey and living at the Woodland Wildlife Center, and he was so proud of his new home that he was always asking people to visit.

I'd been three times so far. The Woodland Wildlife Center was amazing, and I really liked Trevor and Tracey too. The best thing about them was that they were so perfect for Sam. If I could have magicked up the ideal people for him to live with, it would have been them.

I put my two thumbs up to Sam and he put his two thumbs up to me.

"And I'm finally going to be visiting your house today," Angela whispered to me. "I can't wait!"

"It's nothing special," I said. Although it is special—very, very special. Even if our house on Coven Road wasn't the least bit magical, it would have still been the most special place in the world to me because it's my home.

At the end of the day, Lilith was waiting for me and Angela in her red sports car outside the school gates.

I wanted Miss Rowan to meet Lilith. But when I looked a round, Miss Rowan, who had been standing right behind me just a second before, had left.

"Hello, Angela," Lilith said. "I've been looking forward to meeting you."

"I've been looking forward to meeting you too," Angela said politely. "I love your car." She climbed into the back seat beside me.

"Thanks," Lilith said, and we drove off.

I wished Angela could see the magical Coven Road with its amazing houses and the Ice Palace and the unicorns and floating swings and the fountain with dolphins swimming in it. She'd have so loved it, like I did. But of course she couldn't because she wasn't a witch. So all Angela got to see was the ordinary Coven Road, with its ordinary houses and ordinary, but still very pretty, garden in the center.

"Hello, Bella Donna, have a good day at school?" Mr. Robson asked me as we got out of the car. Mr. Robson lived next door with Mrs. Robson and their dog, Waggy. I tried hard not to laugh. It was so strange seeing Mr. Robson dressed in ordinary clothes. I didn't tell Angela that Mr. Robson usually wore a cloak of real, living, running-about spiders when he was being his magical self. He really was spiderman!

Mrs. Robson had a coat of butterflies, which was even better!

"Yes, thank you," I replied, keeping a straight face. "This is my friend, Angela."

"How do you do, Angela?" he said. "Meet Waggy." Waggy always goes for a walk with Mr. or Mrs. Robson every morning and afternoon.

"Hello, Waggy," Angela said, petting him.

Waggy wagged his tail.

I led Angela up the sidewalk. Because a non-witch was visiting Coven Road all the houses looked the same as each other and Coven Road looked like a perfectly ordinary road of terraced brick houses. The beautiful roses around the door that continually changed color weren't there today.

"Here we are," I said to Angela as we went inside. There was no sign of the cauldron or Lilith's spell ingredients, but everything else looked pretty much the same as normal. Angela's eyes were everywhere as she took it all in. I wished I'd invited her over before.

"These are Mystica, Bazeeta, Brimalkin, and Amelka," I said. The four Siamese cats were sitting in their favorite places on the bookshelves. They looked haughtily at Angela. She petted each of them in turn but they didn't look as if they liked it much.

Angela gave a squeak and then started laughing as Pegatha wound herself around and around her legs.

"Hello, little cat," Angela said, and she crouched down to pet Pegatha too.

"That's Pegatha, and she loves being petted," I said.

Pegatha started to purr.

I'd told Angela lots about Pegatha before. Angela didn't have a cat but she would like to have one.

"Come on, I'll show you my room," I said as Lilith began to make dinner.

We went up the stairs with Pegatha following us.

As soon as we got into my room, Pegatha jumped onto my bed.

Angela laughed. "She's so cute," she said. "She just needs one more thing."

"What?" I said. As far as I was concerned Pegatha was perfect and didn't need anything at all.

"This," said Angela, and she pulled a fluffy pink cat toy on a long ribbon from her pocket.

"Thanks," I said, smiling at her.

Pegatha thought it was the best toy ever and chased after it and pounced on it before letting

it go so Angela could pull it away and Pegatha got to chase it all over again. I think Pegatha must have liked Angela very much for bringing her such a cute toy to play with.

We let Pegatha play with her new toy by herself for a little bit while I showed Angela my witch mobile. I told her how it had been with me when I was left on the steps of Templeton Children's Home as a baby.

Angela was soon inspecting my closet to see if she could find the pink clothes I wore for a while to school. "They must be here somewhere," she said, her head deep inside.

At that moment, Verity burst into my room. "You're in!" Verity yelled.

"What?" My heart was banging away.

"Haven't you been watching Broomstick TV? Your name just came up on the screen! Haggerty and Fizzwart told me to tell you. You're in the Witchling spell-casting contest!"

I couldn't take in what she was saying to start with. Why was she saying all this about magical

 things? Didn't she know I had a non-witch visitor? Why hadn't Lilith stopped her from coming upstairs? Verity must have let herself in and just come right to my room. I opened my mouth to speak but no words came out.

"What?" said Angela, struggling out from the back of the wardrobe. "What was that? I couldn't hear properly in there. You're which what?"

I didn't know what to say. How on earth was I going to explain?

As soon as Verity saw Angela she shut her mouth like a trap.

"I'm Angela," Angela said.

"Verity," said Verity, all smiles. "Bella Donna's cousin."

"She didn't tell me she had a cousin," Angela said. "I wish I had a cousin."

Pretty soon it was like Verity and Angela had been friends for life. That was the effect Verity could have on people—when she wanted to.

I tried not to be jealous, which wasn't too hard. The hard bit was that I kept smiling and smiling to myself. I was so excited about being in the competition. I couldn't keep the news inside for one second longer.

"Back in a minute," I said, and ran downstairs to tell Lilith the good news.

Lilith had almost finished making dinner.

"I'm in it!" I said.

Lilith immediately knew what I was talking about and gave me a big hug. "Congratulations!"

Verity and Angela came downstairs then and we couldn't say another word about the spell-casting contest. It was very difficult when it was all I wanted to talk about!

"Dinner's ready," Lilith said. She took four small pumpkins filled with mushroom and butternut squash risotto out of the oven.

"How did you know I was staying for dinner?" Verity asked.

"Lucky guess." Lilith smiled.

Verity often came to our house for dinner. I didn't blame her—Lilith's cooking was amazing.

"Yum," I said. Mushroom and butternut squash risotto is one of my favorites.

"Yum," said Verity. She loves pumpkin risotto as well.

"This is delicious," Angela said, when she tasted it. "It makes me feel like I'm a little witch when I'm eating it."

We all suddenly stopped, forks halfway to our mouths, and stared at her.

"Because of it being inside the pumpkin," she added. "Like Halloween food."

We breathed a sigh of relief and continued eating.

Pegatha doesn't like mushroom and butternut squash risotto so she gobbled up her cat food instead, the pink toy beside her bowl. I thought it was very sweet that she wanted to take it with her wherever she went.

I caught Lilith's eye, and she winked at me. It was lucky Verity was there to talk to

Angela—all I could do was think about the competition.

After dinner Lilith, Verity, and I dropped Angela off at her house and as soon as we got back I switched on Broomstick TV. Haggerty and Fizzwart were stirring a cauldron.

"Stir the cauldron till it's thick. Stir the cauldron slow and quick," said Fizzwart.

Haggerty looked out of the screen. "Better get practicing, Bella Donna," she said. "The next round of the contest is on Saturday."

"I will," I said.

"And we'll help you prepare," said Lilith and Verity together.

I smiled at them.

Just about every evening from then on, Verity came around to help me revise the spell ingredients that Lilith had taught me. Sometimes I wished

Verity wouldn't come around quite so often. I felt like I had spell ingredients coming out of my ears!

It made it hard to concentrate at regular school because I had spells floating around in my head all the time.

Verity was really kind, offering to help me when I knew she must be feeling a bit jealous that I was taking part in the competition and she wasn't. I know I would have been a bit jealous of her if it had been the other way around. I'd still have helped her as much as I could, though.

One night, I'd had enough, and Verity and I ended up having a pillow fight until Lilith came in.

"She started it!" Verity said.

"No, she did!" I said, grinning.

"It was her!"

Lilith tried to look stern as she told us to stop, but ended up laughing as Pegatha jumped and tumbled, chasing the feathers that had fallen out of the pillows.

Even though I was in the spell-casting contest and would need to cast a spell in the final (if I got through to the final), Lilith was still only allowed to give me one actual spell-casting lesson a week, and I was still only allowed to learn an absolute maximum of one new spell a week. The point was that I needed to be able to cast the spells that I had been taught really, really well. It would be much better to know a few spells extremely well than lots of spells not very well.

I knew the change-what-you-look-like spell already. It was the first one Lilith had taught me and the words were *Eeerooola eeeroolu mooozlar kal*. Or at least, that's as accurate as I can get writing them down. The first time I'd used it I'd given myself long purple hair and the second time I used it to get rid of a nasty rash from a spell Verity cast on Sam, but I'd ended up turning Sam invisible by mistake. Lilith said that was one of the most important things for a witchling to learn—how to control your magic so your spell worked exactly how you wanted it to. Now I had to practice the spell so I could make the smallest of changes, like putting a tiny diamond on my toenail.

I thought it would be easy. After all, I knew how to say the spell and had mixed up exactly the right ingredients for it. But there's still one very important thing you need—probably the most important thing of all—and that's your intention, your will, the power you put behind the spell. That's not so easy to learn and no one else can teach it to you because it has to come from you, and of course everyone is different, and so the amount of inner magic they have

is different too. The first time I tried to do it I
ended up with a great big diamond—bigger than
my whole foot. Verity laughed and laughed.

"You will never win the spell-casting contest
like that," she said.

Lilith gave her a hard stare and Pegatha hissed at her.

"All right, all right, I'm sorry," Verity said. "Can't anyone take a joke in this house?"

"You're one of those rare witchlings who has more power than you need," Lilith said to me. "For most witchlings it is the other way around and they need to build up their power rather than refine it. For most witchlings, their first attempt would have produced only a speck of a diamond, almost too small to see, and then gradually, as they worked on the spell and their inner magic grew, the diamond would grow too."

"Unlike you!" Verity interrupted. "You'd end up with a diamond bigger than you are if you built up your magic any more. You might even get stuck inside it!"

"I'm sorry," I said. Maybe I wasn't going to be able to win the spell-casting contest after all. A spell that was too big, when a witchling needed a small spell, would be just as bad as a spell that was too small when a witchling wanted a big spell.

Lilith patted my hand. "Maybe it's time you went home, Verity," she said.

"I want to stay," Verity said. "Please let me stay. Please, please, please. I promise I won't say another word for the rest of the lesson."

"It's up to Bella Donna," Lilith said.

Verity clasped her hands together in a begging sign to me.

"It's all right, she can stay," I said. Verity had only been telling the truth, even if it wasn't very nice to hear.

Verity pretended she was zipping her mouth closed.

"What will happen if I do the spell too strongly?" I asked Lilith. "What if I end up trapping myself inside a diamond or something, like Verity said?"

Lilith gave Verity a hard stare, and Verity just shrugged.

"What?" I said, not understanding what was going on.

"The spell can actually be used to do that," Lilith said. "It's only used to trap a bad witch, though, and they're encased in amber rather than diamond."

"And it'd be the same words as I just used—but I'd need to be thinking about the bad witch rather than myself?" I said.

"Yes," Lilith said, and she smiled at me. "You'd also need to have at least a tiny piece of amber with you. And, of course, if they had some amber with them—"

"Then they'd be able to reverse the spell?" I said.

"But if they didn't have any—"

"They couldn't."

Lilith smiled again. "You have such a natural instinct for magic, Bella Donna."

Verity frowned.

"You do too," I told her. It must have been so hard for Verity not to be allowed to use magic. I know I would have hated it.

Verity crossed her arms and looked away. I don't think she believed me.

# Chapter 6

As I've said before, my friend Sam and I both used to live at Templeton Children's Home before we were adopted. When we were five, we made a pact that we wouldn't let ourselves be adopted by just anyone, but would wait for the perfect family for us—our Forever Family. My Forever Family turned out to be one person—Lilith. I'd had to wait until I was ten to be adopted by Lilith, and Sam had had to wait a little longer to be adopted by Trevor and Tracey. But Lilith was perfect for me, and Trevor and Tracey were perfect for Sam. Sam must have told me at least a hundred times how pleased he was to be living with them at the Woodland Wildlife Center. And now the whole class was going to meet Trevor and Tracey on our first Homes Project class trip there.

Miss Rowan took attendance and told us to make sure we all stayed together as she didn't want anyone getting lost. It was about a fifteen-minute walk to the Woodland Wildlife Center and everyone was very excited.

Sam complained all the way there because first he'd had to walk to school and now he was having to walk all the way back to his house when he could have just met us there.

"I'm going to have to walk all the way back to school for the afternoon and then all the way back home again—I'm going to be exhausted," he moaned.

Trevor and Tracey came out to greet us when we arrived. They were both wearing baggy, patched-up sweaters and rain boots, as usual, and had rosy faces from spending most of their time outside.

Tracey had made a special juice that everyone was happily drinking until she told us it was carrot and red onion juice. Sam didn't seem to mind, though. He gulped down one glass and then he gulped down a second. Tracey looked very pleased.

After we'd had our juice, Trevor took us around the Woodland Wildlife hospital. They had about ten animals in there. A few of them, like the grass snake, were in glass cages, and a few of them were in normal cages, like the hedgehog with the injured leg and the squirrel that had lost its tail.

"Sometimes Trevor has to stay up all night looking after an animal if it's sick," Sam said.

"It's worth it when I get to release them back into the wild," said Trevor.

Most of the animals weren't sick enough to need to be in the hospital—there were lots of animals outside too.

Some of the rabbits were in hutches but most of them were in a kind of pen where they could run around as they liked. Trevor let us feed the rabbits from a bucket of interesting rabbit treats—carrots, green peppers, spinach, watercress, celery, and dandelions. The rabbits thought the treats were very fine indeed! I liked the way one of the rabbits held the carrot in his paws to eat it. He looked so cute and funny.

"Now it's the deer's turn," Trevor said.

That was when something strange happened. There was a small herd of deer—six or so—in the paddock close to the center. Trevor gave us some food to feed them, mainly apples and carrots from two large buckets, and they came over and started eating. But when I put my hand out with an apple for them, all the deer ran away.

"Oh no, what did they do that for?" Angela said.

"Deer are easily scared," Trevor told her. "Something must have spooked them."

What had I done? All I'd wanted to do was give them some food. I thought I'd done the same as everyone else. A thought crossed my mind. Could they have known that I was a witchling and been frightened of me? I didn't like the idea of that.

Miss Rowan, who was standing behind me, put her hand on my shoulder. "Silly deer," she said.

Later on, something even more strange happened. We were following Trevor and Tracey on a trail through the wood when Angela said, "Look—a frog."

Someone else spotted another frog, then another, and another.

"It's like they're following us," Rajni said, sounding frightened.

"This is amazing," said Sam, excitedly. "I don't know why they're doing that."

Soon there were twenty frogs hopping along behind us and more came to join them.

"I've never seen anything like it," Trevor said in wonder.

"Frogs don't bite, do they?" Angela said, a little nervously.

"Course not, silly," said Sam.

But then, frogs don't usually hop after people, either.

Again, I wondered if it was because of me. Were they following me because I was a witchling? No frog ever had

before. Had I accidentally
cast a spell on the frogs to
make them follow us? It
seemed unlikely. I hadn't even
been thinking about frogs when they'd started
following us.

"In the olden days frogs, or more often toads,
were thought to be witches' familiars," Miss
Rowan said.

"Witches, huh? They don't even exist, do
they?" I tried to joke. "Or at least not any more."

Miss Rowan gave me a weird look. "Of
course they exist," she said.

I told Lilith what had happened
when I got home. "Could it have
been my fault? Could I have scared
the deer and made the frogs follow us?"

Lilith shook her head. "I don't see how it could have been your fault," she said. "It wasn't like you put a spell on them."

No, I definitely hadn't put a spell on them, or a least I didn't think I had.

"What if I did it by mistake?"

"Your spells are showing much better control," Lilith said. "I don't think it was something you did. Besides, animals like you," she said. "The deer wouldn't have been scared of you."

I nodded. Animals did usually like me—Pegatha and Waggy were always pleased to see me. The Siamese cats didn't count. They don't really like anyone apart from Lilith.

"It was probably nothing," Lilith told me. "Try not to worry about it."

But I didn't think it was nothing. I thought it was something. I just didn't know what.

"Our teacher said frogs and toads can be witches' familiars," I said. "What's a familiar, and why are frogs and toads familiars?"

"A familiar is a spirit that usually takes the form of an animal. It helps and supports a witch," Lilith explained.

I stroked Pegatha. "Like a witch's pet?"

Lilith nodded. "Although a familiar is supposed to have special powers of its own."

I smiled. "If Pegatha had special magical powers I think she'd be conjuring up plates of fish and cat treats for herself."

"Most often the familiar turns itself into a black cat—but I don't see why it shouldn't be a striped cat or a Siamese one," Lilith said.

Bazeeta suddenly gave a meow from the bookshelf as if he were agreeing with us.

Lilith and I laughed.

"A familiar can take the form of any animal at all really, but other popular ones are a dog, or an owl, or as your teacher said, a frog or more often a toad."

"I think Pegatha is a pet rather than a familiar," I said as she settled down to sleep on a cushion.

"Me too," Lilith agreed.

After dinner I was practicing some more spells by myself, when Lilith gave me a present.

"I thought you might like this," she said, and she gave me a beautiful orangey-colored pendant with flecks of black in it. "My mother gave it to me when I was your age, just after I'd started spell-casting lessons. I want you to have it now. Perhaps it will bring you luck in the contest."

"Thank you," I said. "It's lovely."

"It's made from amber," said Lilith, as she helped me put it on.

I admired it in the mirror. I liked my new pendant very much indeed.

"It suits you," Lilith said, smiling.

It was so lovely, I was going to wear it all the time. If it brought me good luck, even better!

# Chapter 7

Finally, Saturday came and it was the day of the next round of the spell-casting contest. Thirteen witchlings had been chosen to take part, and I was one of them!

I was so excited I could hardly sleep the night before. I wanted to make Lilith proud. I wanted to be the best witchling spell-caster for her, and I wanted it for me too. I loved spell-casting. I loved magic and being a witchling and living on Coven Road, and I wanted to show everyone just what it meant to me.

In this round, the contestants would answer questions about spell ingredients. I'd learned as many as I could—but it was impossible for me to know all the possible spell ingredients because there are thousands of them and I hadn't been learning for very long.

Verity came by in the morning and we switched on Broomstick TV. I was wearing my lucky amber pendant, of course, and a new black top Lilith had bought me. Haggerty and Fizzwart came onto the screen and because of the magic of Broomstick TV they could see all thirteen witchlings in their own homes at the same time—although I could only see them. It was time! I tried to pretend I wasn't scared but inside I was terrified.

"Morning, witchlings," said Fizzwart. "It's a quiz today. Don't look away."

Haggerty threw some dried herbs through the TV screen, and they landed on my lap.

Lilith squeezed my hand. "You can do this," she said.

"No helping," warned Haggerty.

"Cheaters will be weepers," said Fizzwart. But I didn't need help. I knew what the dried herb was.

"It's rosemary," I said.

"Maybe it is, and maybe it isn't," said Fizzwart, but I knew that it was.

"Well done," Lilith whispered to me.

"No conferring," snapped Fizzwart.

Lilith squeezed my hand again and mouthed "Sorry" at me.

"All the witchlings have now answered correctly. Time for the next item," said Haggerty.

A bundle of different dried herbs tied together with a ribbon flew out of the screen and into my hand. It was a smudge stick. They're used in special ceremonies to cleanse negative energies—called smudging. The smudge stick is lit during the smudging ceremony and if it was a room that was being cleansed then the smudge stick would be carried clockwise all around the room, making sure you didn't miss any of the corners and behind the door.

"What's in the smudge stick and why?" asked Haggerty.

I looked at the different herbs and tried to smell their different aromas. "Sage for cleansing, thyme for purifying, and mint for energy," I said. "Very good, little witchling," said Haggerty.

"Three witches must go, only ten witches know," announced Fizzwart.

I was so nervous I didn't even have time to think about the amazing fact that I was down to the last ten.

Next out of the screen came yellow brimstone, which is another name for sulfur, and then more plants—coltsfoot and mugwort. I knew all of them, thanks to practicing with Lilith and Verity.

"Nine witches gone, four still along," said Haggerty.

"One more witchling must go," said Fizzwart. "Who will it be—just wait and see."

The last herb to come out of the screen was a fresh plant—bright green with a circular, almost kidney-shaped, leaf.

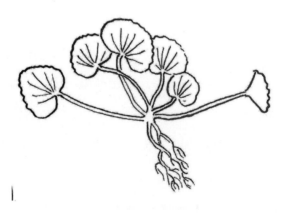

At first I wasn't sure what it was. Did the other three witchlings know? Was I the only one that didn't? It must have been a tough one, because Fizzwart gave us all a clue.

"When your brain doth need a boost, this one's good and that's the truth."

Now I knew what it was!

"Brahmi," I said. The leaves of the brahmi are useful in improving memory.

Stars danced around the TV screen and spun out into our room for Pegatha to try, unsuccessfully, to catch.

"And so we have our final three," said Haggerty.

One of the four of us had got it wrong. But it wasn't me. I knew I'd got it right because of the dancing stars. They wouldn't have been dancing if I'd lost, would they? That would have been mean.

"This year's final contestants are Jezelda Fey, Morgana Fey, and Isabella—known as Bella Donna—Sorciere."

"You did it!" Lilith said. "You answered all the questions correctly!"

"I never thought you would," said Verity.

"No, especially not that last one," said Lilith.

"Would they have let her through if she'd called it Indian pennywort?" asked Verity.

"Excuse me, I am still here," I said. But I was so happy I didn't mind that Verity was showing off. I had a big grin on my face. I'd done it! I'd really done it. I could hardly believe it. And then we were all hugging and Verity was patting me on the back.

"I'm in the finale! I'm in it!" I kept saying over and over.

I was still smiling when I went back to school on Monday morning.

"What are you grinning about?" Sam asked me when I came into class.

"I'm in the finale of the spell-casting contest," I whispered to him.

Sam put two thumbs up. "I knew you could do it. You really are amazing at spell-casting, Bella Donna."

"Thanks."

Sam was the only non-witch I could tell about being in the spell-casting contest, of course. He knew how important it was to me but we hardly ever spoke about anything witch-related at school—just in case anyone overheard.

Miss Rowan announced that today was the day we were going to Rajni's dad's restaurant. Rajni's dad had invited our class to visit after he'd heard about us going to the Wildlife Center. Everyone clapped when she told us. Rajni blushed.

Just about everyone in our class had been to Rajni's dad's Indian restaurant at one time or another, for birthdays and other celebrations. It was really popular.

Rajni's dad was small and very round. "I opened this restaurant because I love to cook," he told everyone and then he laughed and patted his stomach. "And because I love to eat good food."

He showed us the restaurant's kitchen, which was much bigger than the one at school and very shiny. "I like to put lots of spices in my food," he told us.

He held up a dried fruit that looked like a star.

"Who can tell me what this is?" he said.

I knew what the star was, of course, but I didn't want to draw attention to myself by saying anything. I'd seen it used in the monthly midnight spell. It was meant to ward off evil, and so help protect Coven Road.

"No one?" said Rajni's dad, looking around at us all. "It's called anise. Star anise."

"It smells lovely," Angela said.

Miss Rowan gave a giant sneeze and stepped back.

"Bless you," I said. "Are you okay?"

"I'm fine," she said, but she looked a little pale.

"It's good for freshening the breath too," said Rajni's dad.

Then he showed us lots of different herbs and spices and other flavorings he used in his cooking.

"What about this one?" Rajni's dad said, holding up a bunch of dried flowers. "I bet you wouldn't expect to find it in my kitchen. Go on—smell it," he said to Sam. "Do you know what it is?"

"Lavender," Sam said.

"Yes."

"Very popular with bees," Sam added.

"And very delicious in ice cream," Rajni's dad told us, and he gave us all a small bowl of lavender ice cream to try. It was yummy.

When I got home from school I told Lilith about our visit to Rajni's dad's restaurant and the delicious lavender ice cream we'd been given to taste.

"Lavender is very powerful," Lilith said. "It can be used for cleansing, protecting, and strengthening—or all three."

"It tastes nice too!"

Lilith smiled. "You really seem to be enjoying school at the moment," she said.

I realized she was right. Since Miss Rowan had come along, school was fun—lessons I understood, lots of field trips . . . I wondered how long she would stay for. How long would we have before school became hard and boring again? I liked Mrs. Pearce, but I hoped Miss Rowan would stay teaching us forever!

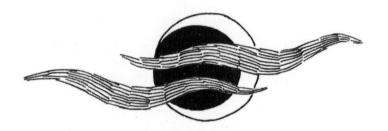

# Chapter 8

It was the day of the spell-casting contest finale and I'd never been so excited or so nervous in my life. I'd spent ages trying to decide what spell to cast, and checked the ingredients I was taking with me about a hundred times since breakfast.

"You'll be fine," Lilith said. "Just do your best." She grinned at me, and I grinned at her because neither of us could really quite believe that I'd managed to make it this far—but I had.

Verity came over just before we were about to leave. "Please, can I come too?" she asked.

"It's up to Bella Donna," Lilith told her.

I didn't really want Verity to come with us, but she had been helpful and she was making an effort to be nice, so I couldn't say no without being mean.

"Okay," I said.

I wanted to take Pegatha too, as my lucky mascot, but Lilith thought it would be better if I didn't. So I gave Pegatha a pat on the head, picked up my bag of ingredients, and then we got into the car.

Broomstick TV was filmed at Walpurgis Castle.
It was even more gloomy and mist-shrouded in
real life than it was on TV.

We had to drive over a wooden drawbridge across the moat and then under a portcullis to get to it.

Luckily, Fizzwart and Haggerty were waiting in the courtyard to greet us. They were wearing heated rollers in their hair, and normal clothes.

"Welcome, welcome!" Fizzwart said.

"Good to meet you in the flesh at last," said Haggerty.

Both Fizzwart and Haggerty seemed very nice and looked pretty normal without their crone make-up and costumes on. They showed us inside, to a room where the other contestants were waiting. Morgana and Jezelda were identical twins and they were a bit older than me—thirteen. They were both dressed in black and had long dark hair in braids. Morgana had two braids and Jezelda had one. They weren't exactly unfriendly but they were definitely a bit aloof.

I was sure that neither of them thought I was going to be much competition for them. They'd lived in a coven their whole lives and so had their parents and grandparents and great-grandparents before them. But just because they'd had more time to pick up knowledge, I knew I couldn't let that distract me. I had to do the best I could.

Before we knew it, we were taken into the main hall that was used as the studio. It had creepy pictures and stuffed animal heads mounted on the walls. I didn't like it at all, but it was very atmospheric!

"Just pretend you can't see the cameras," Haggerty told the three of us, as we stood behind our cauldrons. That was a lot easier said than done. It was very, very hard to pretend the cameras weren't there, filming everything we did. Or to ignore the thirty or so witches and witchlings sitting on dusty maroon velvet chairs in the audience.

"Two minutes to show time!" Fizzwart called out.

The theme tune started to play. I looked out at the audience and saw Lilith sitting next to Verity in the front row. That made me feel a bit calmer.

The show was live, so any mistakes we made would be seen by all the other covens as well as the live TV studio audience that was watching. It was an awful lot of pressure and if I hadn't been able to see Lilith I would have run back to Coven Road as fast as I could.

"When the bell tolls you are to take turns to create your spell from the ingredients you've brought with you," Haggerty said.

"You'll only have five minutes before the bell rings again and you'll have to stop, so make good use of your time," cackled Fizzwart. "Remember it's the quality of the spell you cast that is important."

The bell started to toll.

"Spell time!" shrieked Fizzwart.

"Bella Donna first," said Haggerty.

My hands shook as I dropped the ingredients into my cauldron and stirred. I'd decided to cast the first spell I'd ever been taught—the appearance change spell.

I concentrated hard.

"*Eeerooola eeeroolu mooozlar kal.*"

The first time I'd done the spell I'd turned my hair purple. This time I turned my hair into a rainbow of ever changing colors and it gradually grew longer and longer until it was all the way down to the ground and then it spread out like a rainbow sea across the floor.

It had worked much better than I'd even dared to hope!

The audience clapped and clapped.

"Well done, young witchling," said Fizzwart.

"A very fine attempt," said Haggerty.

I looked out into the audience. Lilith and Verity had their thumbs up. I grinned at them. But then I stopped concentrating and my new rainbow hair started to shrivel up.

That wasn't supposed to happen! I quickly whispered the reversal spell and my hair went back to the way it usually looked.

My heart was beating very fast. Would it matter that I'd lost concentration? I'd completed the spell before it went wrong. But would it count against me?

"Morgana next," said Haggerty.

"Show us what you can do," said Fizzwart.

And Morgana did. First she dropped the ingredients she'd chosen into her cauldron and then she stirred it and said the words, which sounded like "*Fazaaring fazal fazaaring falal.*"

Suddenly everyone in the audience, plus Fizzwart, Haggerty, Jezelda, and me had a plate in our hands.

"Feeling hungry? How about a sandwich?" said Morgana, and sandwiches started hopping out of her cauldron and landing perfectly on people's plates.

I bit into mine. It was peanut butter and apple—one of my favorites. I wondered if it was Morgana's favorite too. Did everyone have peanut butter and apple sandwiches?

Then I heard Jezelda say, "Mmm, Marmite."

And Haggerty said, "I do like a nice cheese and tomato."

"Well done, young witchling," said Fizzwart. "A fine spell, executed well."

"Very tasty too," Haggerty added.

Morgana smiled.

Last of all it was Jezelda's turn. Jezelda's

spell had two parts to it. She dropped a few ingredients into her cauldron and chanted the words, "*Beyoora bandee beyoora bazee.*"

An egg floated out from her cauldron and hovered in the air. It wasn't an egg like you might have for breakfast; it was much bigger than that. It was larger even than an ostrich egg. Larger even than four ostrich eggs, and it was black with flecks of gold on it.

Jezelda added more ingredients to her cauldron and chanted what sounded like a really hard spell to learn: "*Eezaba arooba eebanda yooreeba.*"

The egg cracked and a tiny purple dragon's head peeped out. The audience gasped, and so did I. As we watched, the dragon grew larger and larger until it was about the size of a small pony. Jezelda climbed onto the dragon's back and it took off into the air, flying around and

around the TV studio, swooping and looping, before finally coming to a stop beside Haggerty and Fizzwart.

"Well, I never . . ." said Haggerty. She was clearly as surprised as the rest of us.

"I wouldn't have thought it even possible for a witchling," said Fizzwart.

The audience clapped and clapped and clapped. Jezelda's spell had been truly amazing!

Fizzwart was holding a giant gold cup.

"This year's Witchling Spell-Casting Champion is . . ."

She paused and the pause seemed to last forever. I didn't think my spell had been as exciting as Jezelda's or Morgana's, and of course it hadn't lasted quite as long as it was supposed to, but it was a hard spell to do. I was a very new witchling compared to Morgana and Jezelda. Maybe . . .

". . . Jezelda Fey," Fizzwart said.

I tried not to feel crushed. Jezelda's spell had been very, very good indeed. She deserved to win. It was just—just so hard to accept. Spell-casting was the only thing I'd ever been any good at. This had been my chance to shine—and I hadn't.

Jezelda went to collect her cup. She looked really, really happy, like I would have if it had been me that had won. But I knew I didn't deserve to win it, not this year. Jezelda had beaten me fair and square.

Haggerty held up a smaller cup.

"This year's runner-up is . . ."

It couldn't be me, could it? Even though I was sure it couldn't be me I really, really wanted it to be.

". . . Morgana."

I clapped for Morgana. She didn't look as ecstatic as Jezelda had done for coming in first, but she still looked very happy.

I couldn't look out at the audience. I hoped Lilith wasn't terribly disappointed that I'd let her down. I was so disappointed in myself. Disappointed enough for the both of us.

Fizzwart was holding a small shield.

"And last, but not least,

we'd like to present this to Bella Donna—our most promising newcomer."

The audience clapped as I went to collect the shield.

"We hope to see you again next year," said Haggerty.

I'd so wanted to make Lilith proud of me. I'd wanted her to see what a good witchling I was and how good at spells I was.

"I'm sorry," I said, when the show was finally over and she came up to me. I bit my lip because I was desperate not to burst out crying. My voice cracked a little but it was so noisy in the studio that I don't think Lilith noticed.

Verity did though. She looked really sad for me.

"Sorry for what?" Lilith asked me.

"Not winning the spell-casting contest."

Lilith gave me a hug. "Oh, Bella Donna," she said. "I don't care about that. Don't you know that to me you already are the best?"

"Am I?"

"Yes, you're the best daughter as far as I'm concerned, and that's all that matters. No amount of spell-casting contest winning or losing is ever going to change that."

"It won't?" A tear slipped down my face, and then another tear followed it and another.

Lilith hugged me again. "No, it won't."

# Chapter 9

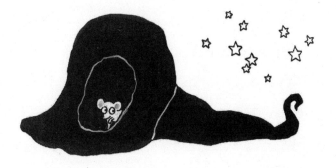

"How did you do?" Sam asked, as I went through the school gates on Monday morning.

"I came in last," I told him.

"You did?" Sam said. He sounded surprised. "But you're so good at spell-casting."

"Not good enough to magic up a dragon yet," I said.

"A dragon!" Sam looked wistful. "I'd have really liked to see that."

The bell rang. It was time to go in.

"How big was it, exactly?" Sam called after me.

Even though Lilith had said it didn't matter to her that I hadn't won, not one tiny bit, I was still feeling miserable.

"You okay?" Angela asked me in class.

I couldn't tell her what was wrong. "Fine," I said. But really I felt like I had a gray cloud hovering over my head that went everywhere with me, and it still hadn't gone by the end of the day.

I trudged home, telling myself it really didn't matter about the contest. There'd always be next year. But I couldn't shrug off my sad mood however hard I tried. Then I heard a noise coming from a car parked just ahead of me.

"Hello, Bella Donna," said a voice. It was Miss Rowan!

"Miss Rowan, what are you doing here?" I asked her.

"Hop in, and I'll give you a ride home," Miss Rowan said.

I couldn't do that. "No, it's okay. I don't have far to go," I told her.

But Miss Rowan wouldn't take no for an answer. "Get in. I want to talk to you about your schoolwork," she said.

I wasn't sure what to do. I was nearly at Coven Road. The turn was just up ahead, but thanks to the monthly midnight spell she wouldn't be able to see the entrance to the street—non-witches can't see it unless they are expected visitors. Wouldn't she think that was a bit odd when I asked her to stop?

*Should I try running away? I'm quite a fast runner but I'm not faster than a car. Perhaps I could pretend I was going to Angela's house, although she didn't live anywhere near me.*

Anyway, I felt bad. Miss Rowan was only trying to be helpful. Maybe I should just get in the car. We could talk about my schoolwork, and then I could get out of the car and walk home.

I'd almost decided to do it. I'd even lifted my foot to take a step toward the car when something changed.

She suddenly didn't seem like the sweet teacher I'd gotten used to. She even started to look different. She was still Miss Rowan but not the same Miss Rowan. I began to feel frightened.

Miss Rowan got out of her car and it was like looking at a stranger. Nothing big had changed, but her eyes were mean and her face was hard and had a big scowl on it.

"I've had enough of this. Take me to Coven Road, right now!" she demanded, in an angry voice.

"I—I . . ."

Now her face started to look really different. Her nose grew, her teeth became pointed and so did her chin until she looked like—well, she looked like an evil witch.

She saw my frightened face and gave a truly wicked cackle.

And suddenly I knew what must have happened. I just knew. All those times I thought I'd cast a spell by mistake—Mrs. Pearce going missing, pink cake and custard, even the animals behaving oddly at the Woodland Wildlife Center—none of them had had anything to do with me. They were all Miss Rowan's doing.

"It was you," I said. "You're a witch!"

Then I realized something very worrying. Miss Rowan had reacted badly to the star anise, which protects against evil. *And* she obviously wasn't able to see Coven Road, which all witches are able to do . . . unless . . . unless she was a bad witch that Zorelda didn't want to let in.

While I was thinking this, something even more strange and frightening happened. Miss Rowan started to chant a spell: "*Kayaaakata koo . . .*"

I didn't know what the spell would do to me, but I had a strong feeling it wouldn't be anything good. I tried to chant one back at her, to protect myself. "*Eeeeuorulo . . .*"

Miss Rowan laughed. "You think your feeble witchling spells will work on me? Foolish girl."

I began another spell, "*Lanuuus . . .* um *. . . oooma.*"

"There's no point in trying that," Miss Rowan sneered. "I've protected myself against every counterspell a witchling at your level might know."

I was so scared that I felt sick. There was nothing I could do. I wasn't strong enough to fight against her spells. I was just a witchling, and a new witchling at that.

"*Kayaaakata koor kayaakata roo . . .*" Miss Rowan began chanting again.

And although I didn't want them to, and I tried my best to fight against it, my legs started walking toward Miss Rowan's car. I grabbed a hold of a street light to try and stop myself from moving, but that didn't work. One by one, my fingers let go of their hold on the street light, even though I didn't want them to at all.

"Help, help!" I cried.

"Leave her alone!" a familiar voice shouted. It was Verity! She was racing down the street toward us.

Miss Rowan pointed a finger at Verity and chanted a new spell at her.

"Ow!" Verity cried and she started to hop as if someone had stuck a sharp needle in her foot.

Verity tried to do a counterspell back at Miss Rowan but it didn't work either.

"Ow!" This time Verity grabbed her arm as if someone had stuck a big needle in it.

I got even more scared. So scared that I was shaking with fear. It would be almost impossible for witchlings like Verity and me to beat an experienced witch.

Verity grabbed my arm and tried to stop me from getting into the car, but it was no use. My legs kept moving me toward the car door even though Verity kept trying to pull me back.

Terrified, I closed my eyes and buried my chin in my chest, waiting for whatever awful thing was going to happen to us. And that was when I felt something hard against my chin. It was the amber pendant Lilith had given me! What did I have to do

to cast the entrapment spell? I hadn't exactly been
taught it, but Lilith had spoken about it. I tried very,
very hard to remember the words—and suddenly

I did! I wrapped my fingers around the pendant, whispered the spell, and tried really hard to imagine Miss Rowan inside a giant piece of amber.

Verity gasped and I opened my eyes. There, in front of us, stood Miss Rowan—and she was trapped in an amber shell with an expression of pure fury on her face.

She wasn't the only shocked one. I almost fell over when her spell stopped working on me and my legs were released. My body was mine again!

"Quick!" Verity said. "We need to get help before the spell wears off."

We ran along the street to the turn, then raced, shouting, all the way up Coven Road to the Ice Palace and banged on the big front door.

"Zorelda! Zorelda!"

The door swung open on its own and we hurried inside and almost bumped straight into the Grand Sorceress.

"What is it?" Zorelda said, looking at our panicked faces. "What's wrong?"

I'd run so fast it was hard to catch my breath.

"Someone tried to break into Coven Road," Verity said. "Bella Donna stopped her. She trapped the witch in amber . . ."

"But we don't know how long it will hold her," I gasped.

Even as we were talking, Zorelda was hurrying out of the palace with us close behind. "Take me to her," was all she said.

A few minutes later we'd reached the car.

"Aha," said Zorelda. "Rosina Rowan, up to your old tricks again, I see."

I was very surprised Zorelda recognized her.

"You horrible little girls," Miss Rowan said, her eyes shooting daggers at me and Verity. Her voice sounded funny, and she didn't seem to be moving her mouth when she spoke.

"Rosina Rowan has been expelled from just about every coven in the country, apart from

Crone Close, and no one would want to live there," Zorelda told us. "You've done a very good job in holding her. I put a spell on Coven Road to keep bad witches out, but if she had got in, if she had managed to force you to bring her in . . ." Zorelda shuddered. "If she'd got into Coven Road she could have caused all sorts of trouble. She may even have managed to destroy Coven Road completely."

Destroy Coven Road? I couldn't even bear to think about it.

"She's been trying to find a coven that was weak enough for her to take over for years," Zorelda told us.

"I'll make you sorry," Miss Rowan sneered at Zorelda. "You think you're so powerful but you're not—you're just—"

I never did get to hear what Miss Rowan was going to say next because Zorelda started to chant what must have been a very powerful spell. "*Xiara xielda zalood remar xiara xielda zalooda zala . . .*"

"Nooooooo!" Miss Rowan cried.

But it was too late. There was a clap of thunder, and Miss Rowan disappeared. No amber left, nothing, just a blank space where Miss Rowan had been.

"What have you done to her?" I asked. I'd liked Miss Rowan. I'd liked her a lot, and even though I now knew she was bad and out to cause trouble I didn't want anything too horrible to happen to her. Zorelda was very powerful.

"I've sent her back to the only coven where she's welcome," Zorelda said. "Crone Close. Let them reverse the spell. A day or so trapped in amber won't do her any permanent harm."

The Ice Palace bell rang and soon all the witches of Coven Road were assembled to hear Zorelda's announcement.

"Today, Coven Road has been saved from the certain danger of Rosina Rowan by our newest resident, Bella Donna," she told everyone.

There were gasps at the mention of Rosina Rowan's name and everyone clapped and cheered when they heard that her plan to get into Coven Road had been thwarted.

"If you hadn't cast your spell Rosina Rowan would have got into Coven Road for sure," Verity said, as the clapping continued.

"But if *you* hadn't come along, I wouldn't have had the chance to cast the spell," I said.

Working together we'd been able to stop Miss Rowan. We smiled at each other.

"Bella Donna and Verity have proved themselves to be worthy witchlings," Zorelda said, once the clapping had died down. "And Verity . . ."

"Yes?"

"The ban against you is lifted."

Everyone clapped once again. Now I could see Lilith in the crowd. She was smiling at me and Verity.

"Thank you," Verity said to Zorelda. "Thank you so much."

I smiled at Verity. I knew how much this meant to her. She deserved it. Without her . . . I don't know what would have happened.

"Well done, Verity," Lilith said afterwards.

"Now I can take part in the spell lessons again, can't I?" Verity said.

"Yes, you can," Lilith said.

"I missed doing magic *sooooo* badly," Verity said.

"I know you've been upset that you didn't win the Witchling spell-casting contest," Lilith said, as we walked home. "But that was just a competition—it wasn't real life. I'm so proud of you and what you did today."

I could feel my face blushing.

"It was very brave of you to put a spell on Rosina Rowan. Most witchlings—and even witches— would have been too frightened, or would have been panicking too much to think about it clearly enough to cast a spell," Lilith added.

"I had to protect our home," I said.

It was as simple as that.

When we opened the door to our house, Pegatha pounced on my bag as if it were a mouse.

"Pegatha, leave my bag alone," I said.

Pegatha sat back, then looked at me and then at the bag and meowed.

"What have you got in your bag?" Lilith asked me.

"Only books and my pencil case," I told her and I opened my bag so Lilith could see what was inside it. "Nothing a cat would like."

That's when Pegatha tried to jump *into* my bag.

"Pegatha, stop it!" I said.

"Maybe put your bag in your room where she can't get it," Lilith said.

I went up the stairs, with Pegatha following me all the way. When I opened my bedroom door and put the bag on my bed, Pegatha jumped on the bed too.

"No, Pegatha," I said, and I carried her back down the stairs. "My bag isn't for you to play with."

As soon as I put Pegatha down she ran back up the stairs. But my bedroom door was closed and she couldn't get in, so she curled up and went to sleep outside my room instead.

After a yummy dinner of wild mushroom soup with rosemary bread, I went upstairs to do my homework and that was when I saw there was a toad sitting on my pillow!

I gave a shriek and the toad croaked, "It's me."

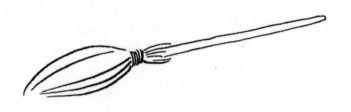

# Chapter 10

I'd know Sam's voice anywhere, no matter what he looked like.

"Sam? What happened?" I asked.

"I've been turned into a toad! *Croak*."

Well, I could see that for myself. But who would have turned him into a toad?

"One minute I was me and the next minute I was thinking a fly would go down nicely. *Crooooaak* . . ." Sam's new long tongue flicked in and out. "Got any flies?" he asked.

"No," I told him.

"I really like flies."

Surely he shouldn't have been thinking about flies at a time like this. Surely he should have been thinking of ways to stop being a toad.

"But what happened?" I repeated. "Tell me everything."

This time he told me. I should have guessed that Miss Rowan would be behind it.

Sam had never really liked Miss Rowan and she had never really liked him. Sam was very suspicious of her and had started to spy on her. Today, he'd spotted her, parked near Coven Road.

He told me, with a few croaks, what had happened next.

"I said to her, 'Where are you going, Miss Rowan?' *Croak*. And she said you'd forgotten one of your books and she was trying to find Coven Road to give it to you. Only I knew she was lying. I don't know how I knew, I just knew. *Croak*.

"'You could give me the book and I'll give it to Bella Donna,' I said. And that's when she started to get very interested in me. She grabbed my wrist really hard and asked me if I'd been to

Coven Road. I didn't want to lie and say no but I didn't want to say yes because I'd promised I wouldn't tell anyone about Coven Road—*croak*—and I keep my promises, so I didn't say anything and that made Miss Rowan really angry. She shook my arm and told me I'd be sorry if I didn't tell her, but I still wouldn't say anything. That's when you came around the corner and I guess she didn't want you to see her nasty side—*croak*—because suddenly I was tiny and green and in her hand and the next instant she put me in her pocket and I could hear her talking to you. *Croak*."

Sam had been there all the time and I hadn't even known.

"I tried to warn you but talking's not so easy, at first, when you've been turned into a toad. All I could do was croak—*croak*."

Poor Sam.

"Luckily there are some things toads are really good at, like jumping, and even though it was a really long way down I wasn't frightened because I know toads have very strong legs."

I raised one eyebrow. "Spit it out, Sam."

"Anyway, I jumped from Miss Rowan's pocket into your bag . . . and it got a bit foggy after that. I think I might have been knocked about by one of your schoolbooks. You had no idea what was going on . . ."

"Sorry, Sam."

"Even Pegatha knew something was going on—she is one clever cat by the way—but not you."

I opened my mouth to say sorry again, but he continued talking.

"Finally, I was able to crawl out of your bag and onto your pillow, where I was sure you would spot me, but all you did was start screaming like a banshee."

"S—"

"I know, 'Sorry, Sam.'" He sighed loudly, which I'd never heard a toad do before, but then I'd never heard one speak either.

"Miss Rowan deceived everyone at school apart from you, Sam. She must have put a spell on our whole class. I wonder why you weren't affected?"

Toad Sam wriggled about a bit, which I thought was probably a toad's way of shrugging.

Just then the phone rang and Lilith called out, "It's for you, Bella Donna."

I took Sam with me as I went out into the hallway to answer it. It was Tracey at the Woodland Wildlife Center.

"Bella Donna, have you seen Sam? We are so worried about him. He didn't come home from school, and he's late for his dinner, and he's never late for his dinner."

I looked down at toad Sam in the palm of my hand.

"He's here," I said. "But he's just leaving."

"Oh, thank goodness," said Tracey, sounding very relieved indeed. "I was so worried."

I put the phone down. "Time to reverse the spell," I told Sam. "I'll get Lilith to do it."

I think Sam was relieved I wasn't going to do it. He doesn't completely trust my spell-casting—just because I made him invisible once, by mistake.

"Lilith, could you help Sam for a minute, please?"

Toad Sam closed his eyes as Lilith said the spell.

He still had his eyes closed when he turned back into a boy. He looked down at his hands.

"Nice to have you back, Sam," Lilith said.

"It was pretty amazing being a toad," he said, sounding a little bit sad that he wasn't one any more.

"Well, you wouldn't want to stay being a toad forever," I said.

Sam hopped about a bit as he thought. "I wouldn't mind being one for a bit longer to see how far I could jump, and toads don't drink, they absorb water through their skin . . . and it'd be really interesting to know . . ." He stopped. "But I'd rather be me, and I'd rather go home."

"Tracey's really worried," I reminded him.

"Yeah," he agreed. "Better get back. Thanks." He grinned at me. "It's good, isn't it?"

I knew what he meant. "Yes, it is," I said.

We had both only recently found our Forever Families. Although Matron Harrigan and Maisie and the other staff at the children's home cared about us an awful lot, it wasn't the same as having a Forever Family who loved you and got in a panic if you weren't home in time for your dinner.

# Chapter 11

The next day, Zorelda announced that we would be having a party to celebrate Coven Road being saved from Rosina Rowan.

I was very happy—witches' parties are the best parties ever.

"It's a shame Sam and Angela can't come," I said to Lilith. "I'd love Angela to see Coven Road in its magical form—she would so love to see the unicorns, especially the pink unicorn foal."

Lilith didn't say anything, but I heard her a few minutes later on the telephone to Zorelda and then she came back and told me the good news. Zorelda had said that both Sam and Angela could come to the party!

"They can meet the unicorns," I said excitedly, "and ride on a flying carpet and—"

"They can enjoy all of the magical delights they like," Lilith said. "There's just one thing . . ."

"What?"

"Only Sam will be able to remember what happens—he already knows about Coven Road. Angela will have forgotten everything by the time she gets home."

I thought that would be very strange, but I did understand. At least I'd be able to share my secret with Angela, even if it wouldn't be for very long.

I called Angela and Sam right away and both of them said they'd love to come and their parents said they could stay overnight.

Lilith and I went to pick them up in Lilith's sports car.

"I can hardly believe it," Angela said, as she climbed into the back of the car with her overnight bag. "First, I'm never invited, and now, I'm always being invited!"

As soon as Sam got to our house he raced around to the back yard to look at the pond. Lilith was growing some very unusual plants in it, which attracted even stranger creatures. Sam would probably investigate the pond for hours. Every now and again I'd hear Sam shout "I don't believe it!" or "I thought they were extinct!" or just plain "Wow!"

"The lights in your roses are beautiful," Angela said. "I didn't notice them when I visited before. They make it look like the roses are really changing color."

I decided not tell her that the roses themselves *were* really changing color just then.

"Come on inside," I said, and we went up to my bedroom to decide what to wear to the party.

Angela wore a pink dress and pink shoes with a sparkling tiara and bracelet. I chose to wear my favorite turquoise dress because it went well with my lucky amber pendant.

"Time to go," Lilith called up the stairs.

We came down to see Sam in a new shirt and trousers that Trevor and Tracey must have just bought him because I'd never seen them before.

Lilith smiled when she saw the three of us. "You look lovely," she said.

"So do you," I said. Lilith had on a beautiful purple dress.

"This is so exciting!" said Angela.

"Um, Angela," I said. "Before we go there's something I should tell you."

I hoped Angela wasn't going to react too badly. She might not like the idea of me being a witch. She might think it was weird. I hoped she'd still want to be my friend.

"I'm . . . I'm actually a witch—well, a witchling, which is a trainee witch."

"You are?" said Angela. Then a big smile spread across her face. "So that's why you want to wear black all the time."

"Coven Road is a magical place where witches live," I went on.

"So, would you prefer to walk to the party or fly on a magic carpet?" Lilith asked.

"Magic carpet, please," said Angela, her eyes wide with excitement.

I'd been a little bit worried that the witches' party and the magicalness of Coven Road might be a bit too much for Angela. I didn't want her to freak out. I needn't have worried at all. Angela took to magic like a duck to water.

She sat down on the magic carpet with the rest of us and didn't even scream as it sped upward and out of the door.

"Look at that!" she said, as we passed over the house that looked like a mini Taj Mahal.

"I like that one better," said Sam, pointing to the Tarzan house.

Lilith steered us toward the Ice Palace. I liked every house on Coven Road because they were all amazing in their own way.

Mr. Robson was wearing his special coat of spiders and Mrs. Robson was wearing her butterfly one. As soon as Sam saw them he jumped off the carpet, which had almost landed anyway, and raced after them.

"Excuse me, excuse me . . . are they really real?" I could hear him calling.

"Ponies!" said Angela, running over to the little garden. But they weren't ponies. They were unicorns, and they had the little pink foal with them.

"Is it all right if I pet them?" Angela asked.

Lilith said it was. The unicorns were very tame. The older ones put their heads down so that Angela could stroke them more easily and the foal nuzzled his nose into Angela's hand. She looked happier than I'd ever seen her before.

"Hello," said Verity. She was wearing her favorite long red ball gown and looked very grown-up and glamorous.

"You look totally amazing!" Angela said, when she saw her.

"Good evening, my dear. It's a pleasure to meet one of Bella Donna's friends," Zorelda said to

Angela, before moving on gracefully to greet her other guests.

"How sweet!" Angela said, when Zorelda had gone past. I'm pretty sure no one has ever thought Zorelda was sweet before.

Soon there were fireworks lighting up the sky, but not ones that scared animals like ordinary ones do. These were special fireworks. Extra sparkly but with no bangs, just the sound of a thousand beautiful tinkling bells instead.

Sam raced over to us. "I saw a tiny elephant!" he said. "It was no bigger than Pegatha." He pointed to the center garden. "It's in the bushes."

And he raced off to see if he could see it again.

Verity took Angela to try one of the magical swings. They have daisy chains to hold onto and stay up in the air by magic. The butterflies love them and are always flying around them.

As I watched them swing, Lilith came up to me. "Happy?" she asked.

"Very happy," I said.

We took Angela to the buffet table next. "Go on," Verity said. "Any food you can imagine will appear."

Angela screwed up her face in thought. "Pink cheese and pink pickles . . ." A pink cheese and pickle sandwich, made with pink bread, appeared in front of her amazed face.

Sam came to join us as Verity went off to see the rainbow sand dancers.

"I wish Verity was my cousin," Angela said. And for the first time I realized that I was very happy Verity was *my* cousin.

"That was the best party ever, ever, ever," Angela said when we got home.

We left Sam to sleep on the sofa downstairs. Amazingly, Mystica, Bazeeta, Brimalkin, and Amelka came off the bookshelves and curled up with him. He really did have a way with animals!

Angela and I got ready for bed too. "I want to stay on Coven Road forever," Angela said as she crawled into her pink sleeping bag. "I'm telling my mom that we have to move here as soon as I get back." With that she fell asleep.

Angela grabbed me as soon as I went through the school gates on Monday morning. "Thank you so much for inviting me to your party. I had such a good time! Only . . ."

"Only what?" I asked her.

"Only, I can't remember a thing about it and my mom keeps asking me."

"You had a great time," I told her, smiling. "You must come again soon."

Angela frowned as she tried to remember, and then she shook her head. "I can't understand it," she said as we walked inside.

As soon as we got into the classroom we saw that Mrs. Pearce was back.

Sam put his hand up. "Where were you, Mrs. Pearce?" he asked her.

Mrs. Pearce frowned. She looked confused. "Well . . . I, um . . ."

"Were you sick?" Sam asked.

"No—I don't think I was sick . . ."

I suppose it wasn't surprising that she didn't know what had happened—she'd had a powerful witch's spell cast on her.

"It's none of your business, Sam," she said in the end. "Now, everyone get out your math books. It's time for some algebra."

I was worried that now Miss Rowan had left I wouldn't be able to remember how to do algebra any more. But that's where I was wrong. It turned out I could still do it. Miss Rowan might have done a lot of bad things but she had taught me how to understand algebra.

"Very good, Bella Donna," said Mrs. Pearce as she looked at my work. "I can see you've learned a lot while I was away."

Sam put his hand up. "I learned what it feels like to be a toad while you were away," he said, his eyes shining.

The whole class, apart from me, laughed.

Mrs. Pearce smiled and shook her head. "What an imagination you have, Sam," she said.

Sam looked over at me and grinned. We both knew he was telling the truth but no one else would believe us.

The secret of Coven Road was safe.

# Bella Donna

## Coven Road

Most girls dream of being a princess, but
Bella Donna has always longed to be a witch.
The only thing she wants more is to find a
family to take her out of the children's home
where she lives.

But no one seems quite right,
until she meets Lilith.

With Lilith's help, will Bella Donna
be able to make both of her
secret wishes come true?

# Bella Donna

## Join Bella Donna online!

Be a part of Coven Road and
keep up to date with the latest
Bella Donna news.

Find out more about Coven Road,
the characters, download games,
puzzles, activities, and much more!

BellaDonnaOnline.co.uk